Contents

People in the story

Jonathan Pine	a hotel night manager
Freddie Hamid	the owner of the Queen Nefertiti Hotel in Cairo
Madame Sophie	Freddie Hamid's girlfriend
Richard Roper	a famous businessman
Jed Marshall	Roper's girlfriend
Major Corkoran	a man who works for Roper
Frisky	Roper's **bodyguard**
Tabby	Roper's bodyguard
Dr Paul Apostoll	a **lawyer** who works for Roper
Lord Langbourne	Roper's **adviser**
Leonard Burr	the manager of an **agency** that helps **British Intelligence**
Rob Rooke	a man who works for Burr's agency
Rex Goodhew	a man who works for the British **government**
Joe Strelski	a man who works for the **Central Intelligence Agency** in America
Geoffrey Darker	a man who works at the River House
Harry Palfrey	a man who works at the River House

Note about the story

John le Carré (real name David John Moore Cornwell) is a British writer who was born in 1931. During the 1950s and the 1960s, he worked in **British Intelligence***. He stopped this work to write full-time after his third book, *The Spy Who Came in from the Cold* (also in the Penguin Readers series at Level 6), became a bestseller. He has written more than twenty books. Much of his writing is about British Intelligence and the work of its **agents** abroad.

The Night Manager, which was made into a British Broadcasting Corporation (BBC) TV programme in 2016, is about the selling of **drugs** and **arms** around the world, and the countries and people who make huge amounts of money from it. The story is about the **corruption** that comes with that money, not only inside large companies but also in **governments**, **including** the British and American governments. In *The Night Manager*, "the River House", where Geoffrey Darker works, is really MI6 – the home of British foreign intelligence. Whitehall is a street where there are many government buildings and offices.

*Definitions of words in **bold** can be found in the glossary on pages 93–96.

Before-reading questions

1 Read the title of the book. The main character, Jonathan Pine, is the night manager of a big hotel. What does he do in his job, do you think?

2 Have you ever stayed in a big, expensive hotel? Or have you seen one on television? What is life like in these hotels, do you think?

3 Look at the definition of "corruption" on page 94. If we say there is corruption in an organization or government, what does this mean?

4 In *The Night Manager*, Richard Roper sells guns and drugs to people and governments. Have you read any other books or seen any films or TV series about this subject?

5 Look at the definitions for "British Intelligence" and the "CIA (Central Intelligence Agency)" on pages 93 and 94. What do you know about these organizations? What does it mean to be an agent for them?

CHAPTER ONE
At the Queen Nefertiti Hotel, Cairo

Jonathan had often seen her, but he had never spoken to her. She was a tall, dark and beautiful woman of around forty years old. He sometimes saw her getting out of expensive cars outside the Queen Nefertiti Hotel in Cairo, where she lived and he worked. Sometimes he saw her in the hotel dress shops. Everyone called her "Madame Sophie", and they all knew that she was Freddie Hamid's girlfriend. Freddie was one of the three rich Egyptian brothers who owned the Nefertiti. Freddie had once lost half a million dollars in ten minutes, playing **cards**.

"You are Mr Pine, the night manager," Madame Sophie said, softly, as she sat on a chair next to the **reception** desk. It was late in the evening, and there were no other hotel **staff** there. Then she smiled and added, "You are the flower of England."

"Thank you," replied Jonathan, and he smiled back at her. "No one has ever called me that before. How can I help you?"

"I am Madame Sophie from apartment number three," she said. "I have seen you often, Mr Pine. You have careful eyes."

"And I have seen *you*," he said.

"You also sail," she continued. "Freddie took me sailing yesterday. I saw you on a pretty blue boat that had an English flag. Is it yours?"

He laughed. "Of course not! It's Mr Ogilvey's, the **Minister**. He works at the **British Embassy**. How can I help you, Madame Sophie?"

She was quiet for a moment, and then she said, "I would like you to do something for me. But first I must ask you a question. Do you know Richard Roper?"

"I'm sorry, but I don't," Jonathan replied.

"But you must know him!" she said. "He is famous and handsome. He has Arab horses and a big boat, and he does a lot of business in Cairo. He is English, like you, and very **confident** and **charming**."

"I'm sorry," Jonathan said, "but I've never heard his name."

But Madame Sophie was not sorry. Instead she looked pleased. "It is good that you do not know him," she said, and she gave Jonathan a large envelope. "Now, I would like you to copy these private papers for me."

"Of course," Jonathan said, and he led her into a small office behind the reception desk. He switched on the **photocopier** and began putting in the papers as she stood next to him.

As he watched each paper go through, he saw that they were letters from a company called Ironbrand to Freddie Hamid. Then his body went cold. The letters were describing the selling of **arms** – guns and **missiles**.

Madame Sophie was watching him work. "Thank you," she said, when he had finished. "Please put the copies in an envelope and put them in the hotel **safe** with your

name on them." Jonathan did what she asked.

"If anything happens to me – I mean if I die – then please give them to your minister friend, Mr Ogilvey," she said.

"If that is what you want, then of course," Jonathan replied. "How long will the papers stay in the safe?"

"Perhaps a night," she said. "Or two nights. You are here every night, aren't you? I will call you sometimes. Thank you, Mr Pine. Goodnight."

When she had gone, Jonathan went to the safe and took out the envelope. Then he quickly made another copy of the letters, which he put into his pocket. He put the first copies into a new envelope and **locked** them back into the safe.

Eight hours later, he was sitting with Mark Ogilvey in his boat. Ogilvey was his friend, but Jonathan knew that he worked for **British Intelligence**.

"So Freddie Hamid is buying arms from Richard Roper," Ogilvey said in a surprised voice. "He'd do better to continue playing cards."

Two nights later Sophie called Jonathan to her room. He found her standing at the window.

"Please tell me the truth," she said. "Where are the papers you copied for me?"

"They're still in the safe," Jonathan replied.

"Have you shown them to anyone?" she asked.

"No one," Jonathan replied.

"Freddie came to see me," Sophie continued. "Mr Roper telephoned him and told him that other people now know about their business. Freddie is not happy." Sophie turned from the window, and Jonathan saw her face. Both of her eyes were **bruised**, and her mouth was cut.

Then she turned back to the window and stared through it. "'Look at all these people,' I told him. 'Every time someone sells arms to another mad Arab leader, these people have less food. Because it is more fun to have a big army than to feed your own people.' I said to Freddie, 'You are an Arab. Is it right that your Arab brothers should pay for your dreams?'"

"What did Freddie say?" asked Jonathan, looking at her face. Those bruised eyes were turning blue and yellow.

"He told me to stop asking questions," she replied, angrily. "I told him that I would not. Egyptians are *my* people!"

"You have to get out," Jonathan said. "Leave Cairo.

You know what the Hamids are like."

"The Hamids can kill me as easily in Paris as they can in Cairo."

After Jonathan left her he telephoned Ogilvey, but there was no answer. Next he phoned a friend in Luxor. "Is your holiday apartment still empty?" he asked.

Then he called Sophie. "A friend of mine has an empty apartment in Luxor," he said. "You can stay there for a week or two."

There was a short **silence**. Then she said, "Will you come too, Mr Pine?"

Jonathan and Sophie sat next to each other on the roof **terrace** of the holiday apartment in Luxor.

"Richard Roper is the worst man in the world," she said. "He knows the bad people everywhere. He is healthy. He is white. He is rich, and he went to the best schools. He is funny, and he is confident. But he **destroys** things. Why? He does not live on the streets. What is wrong with him? You are a man. Do you know?"

But Jonathan did not know. He was watching her beautiful face with the night sky behind it. He could not stop looking at her, and, when he was away from her, he could not stop thinking about her.

Then she said, "Jonathan, did you tell anyone about the envelope in the safe? Did you show the papers to anyone?"

"No," Jonathan lied, and he felt very guilty. "No, no one. Why do you ask?"

"Because Roper was told about the papers," she said, "by some friends of his in British Intelligence."

———

A few weeks later Jonathan stood in Sophie's apartment. Blood was everywhere. It was on the walls, and the bed and the floor. Sophie lay on the floor with her head on her arm. There were policemen in the apartment. One was on the terrace. Another was looking into her empty safe.

"I loved you," he thought, as he looked down at Sophie's body. "I loved you, and I didn't tell you."

"Were you sleeping with this woman?" asked one of the policemen. He was smoking a cigarette.

"No, we just met for coffee sometimes," replied Jonathan. "She was friends with Freddie Hamid. Do you know Freddie Hamid?"

"No," the policeman said. "Did you kill this woman?"

"Yes, I killed her," thought Jonathan. "But not how you think. I killed her because I showed her papers to Ogilvey, and Roper learnt about it."

"No," he replied. "What are you going to do?"

"It must be a **robber**," said the policeman. "A robber killed her."

CHAPTER TWO
At the Hotel Meister Palace, Zurich

It was a snowy evening. Jonathan and several other hotel staff were standing on the stone steps of the Hotel Meister Palace in Zurich. They were waiting to welcome their guests.

"It must be a different Roper," Jonathan had thought this afternoon when he saw the **list** of guests who were arriving that evening.

> Roper R. O., a group of sixteen, arriving
> from Athens by private plane at 9.30 p.m.

"There must be two Ropers who are **dealers** and live in Nassau," he told himself.

It was the middle of winter, and there were very few guests staying at the hotel. Thick snow filled the air and lay on the ground. The weather was terrible, even for Switzerland. "Maybe Roper's plane will not be able to **land** in this weather," Jonathan thought. But, a minute later, several long black **limousines** drove quietly through the gate, and some men and a young woman got out of the first car. They were all wearing very expensive clothes. The woman was in her twenties and had golden brown hair. She wore a long coat that reached her feet. She did not look like Sophie, but she was very beautiful. Jonathan watched her moving up the steps to the terrace on light feet.

Next to her was a tall man of around fifty years

old who wore a brown **leather** jacket. He was strong, and he had thick hair that was grey around the ears. Several **bodyguards** stood around him as he came to the top of the steps and confidently shook hands with some of the staff. Then he turned to Jonathan.

"I'm Richard Roper," he said, and he took Jonathan's hand in his. He had the lazy voice of a very rich, confident and very charming Englishman. "How do you do? There's a lot of us staying here."

"Good evening, sir," Jonathan replied. "My name's Pine. I'm the night manager."

The group entered the hotel with Jonathan behind them. Roper turned to the beautiful woman, who was looking at some magazines on a table.

"Jed, how are you doing, darling?" he said. "She loves magazines, but I hate them myself."

The woman turned and smiled at him. "I'm fine, darling," she replied.

"Have you been here long, Pine?" asked Roper. "Wasn't here last time, was he, Frisky?"

"No way," said a big bodyguard with small eyes and huge hands.

"Where were you before?" Roper asked.

"Cairo," Jonathan replied. "But I wanted a change, so I came here."

A large man in a big leather coat was coming towards the reception desk. He had lots of **passports** in one hand and some envelopes in the other.

"Where have you been, Corky?" said Roper. "You need to sign for everything."

Suddenly there were people everywhere. They had all come out of the limousines. There were men in expensive evening suits and women wearing gold necklaces and bracelets. A handsome man with blond hair came in with a thin, unhappy-looking woman, followed by another bodyguard.

Corky lit a cigarette and started speaking French loudly to someone on the phone. Then he turned to Roper, who was moving towards the lift and discussing **antiques** with the man with blond hair. "Your friend Apo will meet us on Monday lunchtime," Corky shouted. "We can go to the Kronenhalle restaurant – the food's good there. That OK?"

"No," Roper shouted back. "Too many people. Tell him to come here for lunch." Then the woman, Jed, smiled at Jonathan over Roper's shoulder as they disappeared into the large lift.

At 2 a.m. Jonathan looked at the list of guests on the hotel computer. The blond man must be Lord Langbourne, and the thin woman his wife, Caroline. "Corky" must be Major Corkoran. And there she was, Jemima Marshall, or "Jed", from England.

Next he looked at the calls that Roper had made, and Jonathan wrote down all the telephone numbers. "*Roper knows bad people everywhere*," he remembered Sophie saying.

He picked up the phone. "I'd like to speak to Mr Quayle, please," he said. "Tell him I'm a friend of Mark Ogilvey's in Cairo. We sailed together. I have some information."

A few weeks later Jonathan was waiting in a café in Zurich to meet his new **boss**. After a few minutes Leonard Burr came slowly through the door. He was a strange little man with a northern voice. His clothes were not tidy. But he was very intelligent, and he had a happy wife and children at home.

Burr managed an **agency** that helped British Intelligence. He had watched Roper for years. After Jonathan's phone call to his friend Quayle, Burr wanted him to work for **Operation** Limpet.

"I'm sorry about what happened to Sophie," Burr said. "But Ogilvey had to tell us what you'd told him. We couldn't just watch Roper sell arms to the Hamids. We had to do something. Your Sophie died because she told Freddie Hamid to stop buying arms, not because of Ogilvey."

"She wasn't *my* Sophie," replied Jonathan, too quickly.

Burr decided not to hear him. "So you met Corkoran, and the bodyguards Frisky and Tabby?" he said. "Roper likes his men to be English, and he likes them to have a dirty past. Corkoran signs everything. Roper signs nothing. And he was meeting a man called 'Apo', you say?"

Jonathan nodded.

"His real name is Apostoll," said Burr. "He's Greek, but he lives in America. He's a **lawyer** who works for the **drugs cartels**." Burr was silent for a moment, and then he said, "You and Roper were friendly at the hotel? That's good because he'll remember you, and that will help us catch him. Now, let me buy you lunch, and I'll tell you how we are going to do it."

CHAPTER THREE

Jonathan becomes an agent

Jonathan, the night manager, was now an intelligence **agent**. After their meeting, he did everything Burr had told him to do. He stole all the money in the Hotel Meister's safe the next day and immediately left for London. After long weeks of **training**, he arrived in Cornwall by motorbike on a dark and rainy afternoon. He stopped at the village shop to buy food and introduced himself to the woman there as Jack Linden. Then he rode his motorbike straight to the **cottage** at Lanyon Head. As soon as he had left her shop, Mrs Trethewey called upstairs to her daughter to tell her that a nice young man had come to stay in the village.

The villagers soon started to talk about Jack Linden. They talked about how many languages he spoke and how he walked the hill paths every morning with a bag on his back. They talked about how he was rich and how he liked Marilyn Trethewey, who he spent lots of time with. And they talked about how kind he was to lots of people but never said a word about himself.

A couple of months later Jack Linden was seen in Falmouth talking to a large Australian man in a bar. The two of them were drinking beer and staring at a map. They had bought a boat business, someone in the village whispered, but the Australian man was not good at sailing.

A week later both men disappeared, and suddenly

there were police in the village asking questions about Jack Linden and the Australian. "The police think they were selling drugs," the villagers whispered to each other, "and there was lots of blood found at the cottage. They think that Jack murdered the Australian, but his body hasn't been found. And they say that his name wasn't Jack Linden at all. He's called Jonathan Pine."

Burr was sitting with Joe Strelski in a large Miami hotel room that had no windows. Strelski worked for the **CIA** (**Central Intelligence Agency**) in America; he was also interested in Roper and his **deals** with the drugs cartels.

They were there for the first meeting of Operation Limpet. People from the British **government** were not usually invited to meetings about these kind of operations, but, for something as important as Limpet, the CIA needed them there. Each person arrived quietly and gave their name and job. Katherine Dulling came from the River House. Rex Goodhew, who worked for the British government, was there with a **determined** face and smiled at no one. Geoffrey Darker, a small man with cold eyes, was laughing with a red-haired man.

When everyone was ready, Joe Strelski stood up and spoke for fifty minutes about the three Colombian cartels who had agreed to join together to **protect** themselves against three **threats**. The first threat was the United States, who were helping the Colombian government to fight drugs. The second threat was other cartels, especially in Venezuela and Bolivia. And, thirdly, the Colombian government itself.

"During the last eight years," said Strelski, "different groups — **including** French, Israelis and Cubans — have tried to sell arms to these Colombian cartels. Most of them have been quietly helped to do this by their governments. But the cartels haven't really been interested until now."

Then Strelski turned off the lights and showed them a photograph taken through a window of some men sitting inside the offices of a Caribbean law firm. There were two white-faced men, who Burr recognized from Cayman Island banks, and he was interested to see Major Corkoran, with a pen in his hand and some papers in front of him. Next to Corkoran sat the handsome Lord Langbourne, **adviser** to Mr Richard Roper. And across from them was a large Greek man whose face Burr did not know.

"Who took this photo?" asked an American voice from the back of the room.

"One of our agents," replied Burr.

Strelski began to sound excited. "This photo shows us that the cartels have met with some big arms dealers." Then he pointed to the Greek man in the photo. "We know this man as Dr Paul Apostoll, lawyer for the drugs cartels. The men he's meeting with are friends of Richard Roper. We believe that Roper and the cartels are planning to **exchange** a large amount of arms for drugs."

Strelski sat down, and Rex Goodhew stood up to speak. He was sorry, he said, that they were going after a British man, but happy that both the British and American sides wanted to work together to catch him. "We have to stop the **sale** of arms in a dangerous area of the world, and we have to stop the sale of drugs in Europe," he told them. "We have to catch these men and show the world who they are and what they're really doing."

―――――――

Two days later Leonard Burr was in his office in London. He took a phone call from Rex Goodhew. "The Minister is worried about Operation Limpet, Leonard," Goodhew told him. "He's worried about the cost ― and he doesn't want any trouble in the Bahamas."

"That's rubbish!" shouted Burr. "There is *always* trouble in the Bahamas."

"And are you going to tell our friends at the River House about your new agent?" asked Goodhew.

"No way!" shouted Burr. "I know about Geoffrey Darker and his friends. I know about their houses in Spain and their expensive cars. We can't trust them. You know we can't." And he put down the phone.

Burr turned to a man in his office, Rob Rooke. "We're lucky. Harry Palfrey's an adviser to the government. He works at the River House, and he tells us what Darker and his **team** are doing," he said. "No one can know Jonathan Pine's name. Not even Harry. And Geoffrey Darker must never know who our **source** of information about Roper is."

CHAPTER FOUR
Jonathan saves Daniel

Strelski landed the plane on a small **airfield** that had cows on one side. Around them lay the brown fields of Louisiana. He jumped out of the plane and, with gun in hand, walked towards a small building. Burr followed him with empty hands – he hated guns and did not know how to use them.

"I've told him that you're a doctor," Strelski said. "He doesn't know our names."

The building smelled bad, and it was full of rubbish. The two men sat down and waited. Half an hour passed. It was hot, and their clothes were wet. Then, suddenly, the door opened, and a large man walked in wearing expensive black clothes and a gold necklace. Burr looked at Dr Paul Apostoll. "This is the man who brought us information about Roper's plan," he thought. "He eats with Roper and sails with him, and then he sells Roper to us."

"Meet the doctor from England," Strelski said, and pointed to Burr.

"Hello, Doctor," said Apostoll. "I love your great country. It is good to meet someone who has been to university – a *gentleman*."

Strelski began to ask Apostoll questions. Did anyone know he was at this meeting? What time did he have to leave? When could they meet again?

Then he began asking the important questions. "Are the

cartels still buying the **helicopters**, Dr Apostoll?"

"I am not in the room when they talk about things like that," Apostoll replied. "But Mr Roper will sell them helicopters if that's his plan."

Then he told them about different people and places, and money that was coming into the Caribbean, and the cartels' plan for a new building in Miami.

Then Burr asked him another question. "What's Roper's secret? What does he have that the Israelis and Cubans don't have? Why are the cartels buying arms from him and not them?"

Apostoll did not have a problem answering this. "You must understand that Mr Roper is not an ordinary man," he said. "He is charming and confident, and he has big plans. He is a gentleman."

"And of course you've stayed with him in his beautiful houses," thought Burr. "He gave you good food, and beautiful things. And you liked him because he is English and a gentleman."

"Then Mr Roper told us about the newest and best guns and missiles," continued Apostoll. "He said that our boys were brave and good and they should be protected. And he told us that we could forget sending poor people to other countries to sell drugs, or flying small planes across Mexico to the US. He could organize something better – an easy **exchange** that could take our drugs into all of Europe."

"You mean he's going to sell mountains of drugs across

Europe and kill children, and make millions of dollars from it!" shouted Strelski.

Apostoll did not answer the question. Instead he said, "Mr Roper said that he would pay for the whole deal. We don't have to pay anything – we just give him the drugs, and he gives us the arms. The cartels liked this idea – and they trust him."

"And was Major Corkoran at this meeting?" asked Burr.

"Of course," replied Apostoll. "So was Lord Langbourne. Major Corkoran signed all the papers. But I have told the cartels what your agents told me to tell them."

"And what is that?" asked Burr.

"That Mr Corkoran drinks and takes drugs, has a difficult love life and cannot be trusted. But I don't understand why. If Mr Roper does not want to use Corkoran any more, then he will just find another signer."

"Does Mr Roper know yet that the cartels are not happy with Major Corkoran?" asked Burr.

"I don't know," replied Apostoll. "The cartels don't tell me their thoughts."

Then Burr passed him an envelope. "This is a list of all the bad things Corkoran did before he met Roper," he said. "They include drink-driving, drug taking and stealing money when he was in the army. Please give this extra information to the cartels for us."

After leaving Cornwall on his motorbike, Jonathan drove straight to Bristol and got a job on a ship as a chef.

He sailed to Canada on the ship, sleeping in the **hold** and working long hours.

When he got to Canada, he immediately travelled to a town called Espérance in Quebec and found the hotel that Burr had told him about. The woman who owned the Château Babette, Madame Latulipe, was as strange as Burr had said. Jonathan told her he was Jacques Beauregard, from Switzerland, and that he had lost his passport and could not get work. She agreed to give him a job cooking in the hotel kitchen, and to let him stay in one of the hotel rooms. She did not think about her daughter, Yvonne, who was sleeping two doors away from him.

Jonathan worked for ten weeks at Château Babette and secretly started meeting with Yvonne. They kept it secret because Yvonne's father did not like Jonathan, and because she already had a boyfriend, Thomas Lamont, who was a good friend of her father's. Jonathan learned with interest from Yvonne that Thomas had never had a passport.

Then Yvonne's father learned about the two of them and **punched** Jonathan in the face. The next day Jonathan left the hotel, but he already had a passport in the name of Thomas Lamont in his pocket. He got a job on another ship, and he sailed from Canada to the Bahamas and Hunter's Island.

Richard Roper's boat, the *Pasha*, appeared at the east side of Hunter's Island at 6 p.m. The staff at Mama Low's restaurant, where Jonathan now worked, were ready for it.

Someone had telephoned from the *Pasha* that morning and booked a table for sixteen in the name of Roper.

Jonathan thought about the plan that he had made with Rooke, who Burr had sent to meet him in the Bahamas. He had waited for the *Pasha* all week. But, still, when he saw it sailing towards the island, he felt strange and a little frightened. For a second he thought about running away to the island's only town. Then Mama Low shouted at him to get himself to work "right now!", and he smiled to himself and felt better. He began walking quickly towards the kitchen.

An hour later Roper and his friends were sitting around a large table on the restaurant terrace. Roper was dressed in jeans and a white T-shirt, with a blue jumper thrown over his shoulders. There was loud laughing, and Jonathan turned to see the young woman, Jed, sitting opposite Roper and smiling at him. Her dress had no back, and her beautiful golden brown hair fell over her brown shoulders.

With them were Lord Langbourne and his wife and their three children. Another boy sat next to Jed. He was about eight years old and had dark hair. "He must be Roper's son, Daniel," thought Jonathan.

"*Can't we use someone else?*" he had asked Rooke. But Rooke had said it would only take five minutes. "*What's five minutes?*" Rooke had said to Jonathan. "*Roper loves that child, so we have to use him.*"

Frisky and Tabby were also in the group, and Major Corkoran sat next to them with a large hat on his head.

A band was playing, and a man sang slowly about a girl who could not sleep. Daniel had his head on Jed's shoulder.

Jonathan waited while Roper and his party ate their dinner of seafood. "The men will come up from behind the terrace," he thought. "They'll wait behind the trees."

"Just stay near the kitchen," Rooke had said.

Suddenly there was the sound of a gun. Frisky dropped down, and Tabby told the people around the table to get down. But the two bodyguards did not know where the sound was coming from.

Then Jonathan saw two tall men quietly come out of the trees and begin walking around the group. They took their money and watches and Jed's gold necklace and bracelets.

Jonathan was waiting for this moment. Quickly he ran into the kitchen and picked up a long knife. Then he ran outside again towards the terrace to see the two men pulling Daniel up the path towards him, with Roper following them.

"What do you want? Is it money?" Roper was shouting. "Why won't you talk to me?"

And then Jed shouted, "Bring him back!"

At that, one of the men turned round and shouted, "If any of you follow us, I'll kill the kid, OK?"

The next moment, the two men and Daniel were in front of Jonathan. Daniel was crying loudly. Jonathan stared at the men for a second, and then he screamed and punched the one with the gun. The man fell hard to the ground, and the gun flew out of his hand. Then Jonathan pushed the knife against the other man's neck.

"Run back down the path to your father!" he shouted to Daniel.

"He's broken my arm!" screamed the first man. "He's crazy!"

But Jonathan kept the knife against the other man's neck until he saw Daniel reach Jed. At that moment, the man on the ground picked up his gun and hit Jonathan hard over the head with it. Jonathan fell, and the other man began to kick him in the head. He kicked him again and again, until everything went black.

When Jonathan woke up, the men were gone, and Roper's crowd were all staring down at him. He looked up and saw the faces of Tabby and Frisky, Langbourne and his children, Corkoran, Roper, Jed and Daniel – but they looked strange, like he was looking at them through water. Behind them, he could hear Mama Low saying, "That poor Lamont! Is he OK?" Then Roper was asking, quietly, "Why is he calling him Lamont? He's Jonathan Pine from Meister's: the man who worked for them at night. Isn't he, Tabby?"

"That's who he is, Boss," Tabby agreed.

Roper moved closer to Jonathan.

"You're going to be OK, Pine," he said, quietly. "Help is coming. We'll take you to Nassau in a helicopter and take you to the best hospital. You've just saved my son's life, so you must have the best help that we can get for you."

CHAPTER FIVE
On Crystal Island

Burr and Strelski's agents watched everything that Roper did. They watched his boat, houses, helicopters and cars, as well as his company, Ironbrand. They listened to his telephone calls to and from his people around the world. Then they passed all this information to Burr and Strelski in Miami. But, soon after Jonathan was taken to hospital in Nassau, no more was heard from him, or about him. Rooke had rung the hospital and the receptionist had said, "Mr Lamont is here. He is doing OK." But, twenty-four hours later, Jonathan had disappeared without leaving an address. Roper had also gone, and Apostoll could not tell them where he was.

Everything had gone well until now. The two men chosen for the operation at Mama Low's restaurant were from New York. They had had orders to try to take the boy, let Jonathan win the fight and then disappear. Burr and Strelski knew that the *Pasha* never passed Hunter's Island without stopping at Mama Low's, and they also knew how much Roper loved his son.

The days passed, and still nothing was heard about Jonathan. Should Burr return to London? Should Rooke? Then, one morning, Strelksi was listening to Corkoran on the phone when he suddenly shouted to Burr, "Leonard, listen to this!"

Burr picked up a second telephone and heard Corkoran's voice. "Is that Sir Anthony Bradshaw?" he was saying. "This is Major Corkoran here, one of Richard Roper's friends."

"What do you want?" The voice on the other end sounded tired.

"We've got an important question to ask you about a man called Pine," continued Corkoran. "His first name is Jonathan." Then he gave him some information, including Jonathan's date and place of birth. "The Boss wants to know everything about him," Corkoran added. "And he wants to know it now. But you must tell no one about this."

"Who is Sir Anthony Bradshaw?" Strelski asked Burr, when the conversation between Corkoran and Bradshaw had ended.

Burr smiled slowly. "Sir Anthony Bradshaw is an important English businessman and a **crook**. He used to work with Roper, and they know each other well. He's also much too friendly with some of the people at the River House, like Geoffrey Darker."

Burr had now stood up, and he was laughing loudly. "He's alive, Joe!" he shouted. "Jonathan's alive! You don't ask for information about a dead man. They want him. He's going to be part of Roper's team now."

───────────

When Jonathan woke up, he was in hospital, and Jed was sitting next to him. "Can we call anyone for you, Thomas?" she asked, gently, but he shook his head. Everything hurt – those men had kicked him hard. "But they had to," he thought, "if they were going to make it look real."

"Well, the doctor says that you must sleep lots and lots," she said. And she gave him a glass of water with some pills.

"Thanks," he replied, smelling her hair. "I will."

She put her hand on his cheek. "We really can't thank you enough," she said. "You were so brave."

He slept again, and while he was sleeping he felt himself being moved. There was the sound of a plane's engines as it took off, and he knew that the bodyguards Tabby and Frisky were with him. Then they were in a truck. He remembered looking out of the window and seeing tomato fields, and a factory. There were beautiful-smelling trees, and a swimming pool with lights in it. After that, there was a huge house, like a palace, with a huge stone terrace. Then he slept again. When he woke, he was in a different room, but Jed was still there sitting next to him. He could hear people playing tennis outside, and bright sun came through the open window.

"Where am I?" he asked.

"Crystal Island," she replied. "This is Roper's home."

They talked a little. She told him about her rich family and her brother who, she said lovingly, was an *awful pig*. She told him that, when she was not travelling with Roper, she lived here at Crystal. She asked him about his life, but he told her very little. "You had just that small bag. Is that everything you have in the world?" she asked.

He nodded.

"But someone must love you? Care about you?" she said.

When he did not answer, she started to talk about Roper. "He's away at the moment, selling farms."

"What does he do?" Jonathan asked.

"Oh, he owns a company. Well, everyone does now, don't they?" She smiled at him. "He's a really lovely man. He has lots of farms all over the world – Panama, Venezuela. But we really want to know about *you*, Thomas. What were you doing at Mama Low's restaurant after working at Hotel Meister's? It's *so* different."

"I got bored at Meister's," he replied. "So I decided to travel and see what happened."

"Well, we're very glad you travelled our way," she said. "Roper wants me to fly to Miami for a couple of days, but Corky's here, and *everyone* wants to look after you. And we can call the doctor for you any time you need him."

———

Jonathan stayed in bed and listened to the sounds of the house. He heard cars come and go. He heard horses, children and dogs. The days went by, and the air was hot, wet and heavy.

Then, one morning, Corkoran came. "How are we today, old love?" Corkoran asked, and, although he had his eyes closed, Jonathan could smell last night's wine and this morning's French cigarettes on Corkoran's clothes.

"I'd like to go soon," Jonathan replied, opening his eyes to see the large man standing in front of him. Corkoran's pockets were full of pens and rubbish, and his shirt was wet under the arms.

"*Make them run after you*," Burr had said. "*If you don't, they will get bored of you in a week.*"

"Of course," Corkoran replied. "You can go whenever you want. As soon as the Boss is back. See you tomorrow, old love."

The next day, he was there again, sitting in a chair in the corner and smoking a cigarette. "Sorry about the ciggy," he said. "But it helps me think. Have you ever smoked?"

"A bit," replied Jonathan.

"I've been thinking a lot about you, old love," Corkoran said. "'Is he Pine, or is he Lamont?' I thought."

He waited for Jonathan to speak, and waited and waited. Then he stood up and came towards Jonathan. "The Boss loves you, Pine. I do, too. You saved his boy, so we all want to help you. But he's worried about you, too. You can understand why. Meister told him that, after you stole his money, you left Switzerland, ran away to England and killed an Australian man. Something about drugs and calling yourself Jack Linden. The Boss hasn't told anyone of course – just me – but he's asked me to find out about you while he's away with Jed. You've met Jed, of course: tall girl, very beautiful." Then he touched Jonathan's shoulder, but Jonathan did not answer, because he was asleep.

CHAPTER SIX

Jonathan loses his passport

Corkoran continued to talk to Jonathan in the following days and slowly learned about him. First, he learned how Jonathan's parents had died when he was a child. Then Jonathan told him how he had gone into the army and had been a soldier in Ireland. After that he had gone to college, where he learned to be a chef, and had worked in hotel kitchens before going into the reception side of hotel work. This part of his story was all true. Then they talked about stealing the money at Meister's. "The boss owed me money," said Jonathan. "I had worked many more hours than he had paid me for."

Corkoran asked him about Cornwall and Marilyn, and Jonathan explained how the Australian man had lied to him about selling a boat that he owned. Jonathan did not say what he had done with the body. Then they talked about the Château Babette. He did not say anything about Yvonne, but Corkoran knew about her and her father anyway. Then Jonathan explained that a friend had told him about Mama Low's restaurant and that it might be a good place to work for a while.

The next morning Roper flew back from Miami. "The Boss wants to see you," said Corkoran, and Jonathan, who could walk now, followed him through large rooms that were filled with beautiful art and **antique** furniture.

Finally they came to a room so large that Jonathan felt as if he was falling. Through the tall windows he could see a row of white tables with umbrellas and, behind them, the sea. In the middle of the room was a large desk that was covered with leather. Sitting next to it, dressed in white sailing shoes and a blue shirt, was the worst man in the world.

"Pine!" said Roper. "Well done! Very well done! And well done money for getting you well. That's what money is for. So what was the worst bit?"

He stood up with his glasses on the end of his nose, took Jonathan's hand and looked at him closely.

Jonathan lifted his shoulders. He could hear Pavarotti playing somewhere. "When I was in hospital," he said.

"And what do you want to do now?" Roper asked.

"Go back to Mama Low's," replied Jonathan.

Roper laughed. "I mean what's your life plan? What do you want?"

"I haven't really got a plan. I'm travelling, taking time to relax and think."

"Rubbish!" said Roper. "You don't know how to relax. Neither do I. I mean, cooking, boating, languages, some girl in Cairo, some girl in Cornwall, some girl in Canada. An Australian man dead? So why did you do it?"

Jonathan had forgotten how confident and charming Roper was. "Do what?" he asked.

"Save Daniel," Roper replied. "You kill a man one day

and save my boy the next. You robbed Meister's. Why don't you rob me? Or ask me for money? I'll happily pay you anything you want. This is my boy we're talking about."

"I didn't do it for money," Jonathan replied, and he looked quickly at Roper and then at Corkoran, who smiled back at him. "You've looked after me and been good to me. I'll just go."

"Did you know Freddie Hamid while you were in Cairo?" Roper asked, suddenly. "He's a friend of mine. His family owns the hotel that you were working in."

"I knew his name," Jonathan replied. "I never met him."

"He had a girlfriend, Sophie. Did you ever meet her?"

"She had an apartment in the hotel. Everyone knew that she was Freddie Hamid's girlfriend," replied Jonathan, carefully. "She was killed."

"That's right. Just before you left. Were you sleeping with her?" Roper's voice was still friendly.

"Of course not," Jonathan said, quickly.

"Why 'of course'?"

"I'm not mad. Even if she wanted it. Hamid would kill me."

"It wasn't you who killed her then?" Roper asked and looked quickly at Corkoran. Corkoran was smiling.

"No!" Jonathan replied. "Some people said that Freddie did it. She talked too much, they said."

"Corky can't decide about you, you see," Roper added, looking again at Corkoran, who had now stopped smiling. "He thinks there are things about you that we don't know – and that the police don't know. Have you killed anyone else? What about that man you punched to save Daniel? Have you ever seen him before? Did he often go to Mama Low's?"

"No."

"You've never sailed for him, or cooked for him, or sold drugs for him or his friend?" asked Roper.

"No."

"You see, we thought that maybe you'd started with them – that you were planning to rob us. And then you saw how rich I am, and you decided to change sides. Is that why you punched him so hard – because you wanted me to think that you were a good boy?"

"That's rubbish!" shouted Jonathan. "And, actually, that makes me *very* angry. You should take those words back."

But Roper did not seem to be listening. "Someone with your history? A strange name? Running away from the police because he's wanted for murder and stealing? It would be easy to make a rich British man like you by saving his boy. Can you see what I'm saying?"

"I didn't know those men!" said Jonathan. "I've never seen them before!"

Roper was quiet for a moment. Then he said, "Look, I want you to stay here for a while. Swim, get well. We'll decide what to do with you. We may even have a job for you."

"I just want to go," Jonathan said, politely. He was not acting now. He'd had enough. "I need to be alone," he thought.

"Why?" said Roper, looking confused. "I'll pay you good money. You'll have a nice little cottage on the other side of the island. Horses, swimming, boats. You like those things. Anyway, what will you do for a passport if you go?"

"I'll use mine," Jonathan replied.

A cloud went over the sun.

"Corky, tell him the bad news," said Roper.

Corkoran lifted his shoulders and smiled in a sorry way. "I cut it up, old love," he said. "With all the police looking for you, I had to."

"That was *my passport*!" shouted Jonathan.

"Don't worry," Roper said, calmly. "We'll get you a new one."

CHAPTER SEVEN

Time to rest

Roper kept his promise and gave Jonathan a little cottage on the other side of Crystal Island. It had a small terrace, and steps that went down to the beach.

Each morning, Jonathan swam in the sea, and then he put on his clothes and went for a walk along the beach or through the forest. Sometimes he met Jed there, riding her horse. She was usually with Daniel, or sometimes she was with Roper's other guests.

At other times, Jonathan met Roper, and they ran or swam together, often without speaking. Then Roper usually swam to the beach and walked back to his house.

"You can have any woman here except Jed," Corkoran told Jonathan. "If you sleep with her, he will kill you, and so will I."

"Well, thanks, Corky," Jonathan replied. "Where did he find her, anyway?"

"The story is that he met her at a French horse sale."

"So that's how it's done," thought Jonathan. "You go to France, buy a horse and come back with a beautiful woman. Easy."

But Jonathan could not stop staring at her. He watched her every day and night and told himself how awful she was. He watched her swim, her skin golden in the sun, or laughing with her friend, Caroline Langbourne. He did not like her, but he wanted to be near her. "You've sold yourself to Roper," he shouted at her in his head.

"Sophie sold herself to men, too," he thought, angrily. "But she knew it."

———————

Some mornings, Jonathan climbed a hill away from Roper's house, and carried on up until he came to a row of old houses where no one lived any more. He always walked to the end of the row. There he came to a large metal can that lay on its side. He moved the can and began to dig the ground with a knife. The phone was in a metal box in the ground, put there some days before by Rooke. Jonathan switched it on and called the number. He waited until Burr answered.

"How have you been?" Burr asked.

"How have I been?" thought Jonathan. "I'm frightened. I'm falling in love with a woman who is beautiful but stupid. I'm holding on to my life by my fingers. But this is what you promised me, isn't it?"

Burr wanted to know the names of the people who had visited Roper. There were guests with planes and helicopters, Jonathan told him. There were lunch guests and weekend guests. There were some people who looked after Ironbrand. There was Lord Langbourne and his wife, and a big Italian man. There were some bankers from England, who Burr hated most, and finally Apostoll, the little Greek American, who had recognized Jonathan from Meister's.

Burr listened carefully to everything and told Jonathan about each guest, what they did for Roper and how Roper was using them. Then he said, "Remember what I told you about his office. Don't go in there, Jonathan. It's too much of a **risk**."

In the evenings Jonathan usually had dinner at Roper's house. Sometimes Corkoran was there, sometimes not. "Roper's not very happy with Corky at the moment," Jed whispered to Jonathan, and then she went quiet. She knew that she should not tell him Roper's secrets.

Roper talked on the phone a lot – to the captain of the *Pasha*, or to his antiques dealer in London, or to the man who looked after his horses. There were days when Roper was there and days when he was away "selling farms". He never told anyone when he was going, but everyone seemed happier when he was gone. Most of the time, it was Jed who spent time with Jonathan and asked him how he was feeling. "Oh, Thomas, how *are* you? Any headaches? No? Oh *good*." And it was she who told him about how unhappy Caroline Langbourne was with her husband, Sandy. "He's being a *pig* to her, Thomas. He's always going away and leaving her with the children. It's terrible."

Jonathan began to spend a lot of time with Daniel, too. He often walked or swam with him. One morning, when Jed and Roper were arguing loudly about Langbourne and his wife, he took Daniel to the river and taught him how to catch a fish with his hands.

The next day, Roper, Corkoran and Langbourne flew to Nassau.

"I like it when Dad's away," Daniel said to Jonathan and Jed at dinner. "It's best when it's just us and Thomas. It's more normal."

"Daniel, that's not very nice," said Jed, but she did not look at Jonathan when she said it.

CHAPTER EIGHT

Jed learns the truth

Jonathan had decided to **break in** to Roper's office as soon as he had learned that Roper was leaving Crystal with Corkoran and Langbourne.

On the morning they left, Jed and Caroline went out on the horses with all the children. Since arguing with Roper about Caroline, Jed had been strangely quiet, Jonathan noticed. She seemed to watch everyone a lot more, and she did not say very much.

"I wonder if Caroline Langbourne has told her the truth about Roper," he thought.

He planned the **break-in** carefully, first taking Daniel on a long climb up a hill the day before Roper left and picking some flowers. "Who are they for?" asked Daniel, but Jonathan did not answer.

Jonathan had to go through Roper and Jed's bedroom to get to Roper's office. He entered the bedroom quietly with the flowers in his hand, and a **lock pick** in his pocket. The windows were open, and the room was filled with light. On the table next to Roper's side of the bed lay magazines and books about antiques. There were several notebooks and pens. On Jed's side, he could see the shape left by her sleeping body. On her table lay books about horses, and furniture and houses. There were photos, too, of young people laughing in restaurants, and Roper in a swimming pool.

As he looked down at it all, Jonathan realized that he was not there just to find Roper's secrets. He wanted to know Jed's secrets even more, and what held her and Roper together. He put the flowers in a glass on a table and picked up Jed's pillow, pressing it to his face. He could smell smoke and guessed that she and Caroline were up late last night talking by the fire.

He pushed open the door to Roper's large walk-in clothes cupboard. He looked at the rows of expensive suits and expensive English leather shoes. *"Does Roper go to England much?"* he had once asked Jed. *"Oh no,"* she had replied as if she did not care, but for some reason he did not believe her. *"Money problems or something. Why don't you ask him?"*

The door to the office was in front of him. Roper had locked it of course. Jonathan listened. He could hear cleaners' voices, and the sounds of their work, but nothing else.

He reached for the lock pick and put it into the **lock**. His heart was going very fast. "You're breaking into Roper's office," he kept thinking. "You're using a lock pick and breaking into his office. You're breaking into it now."

The door opened. Nothing had broken, and no one was shouting at him. Then suddenly he heard a car outside. He looked out of the window – but it was just the bread arriving. He heard Burr's voice in his head. *"Don't go in there. It's too much of a risk."*

It was just an ordinary little office for doing deals

and making money. There was no expensive antique furniture in here, just an ordinary desk below the window. On the desk lay a letter signed "Anthony", about his money problems. The words of the letter were angry. "Don't read it; just photograph it," Jonathan told himself. He undid his pen, pulled out the small camera and took a photo of the letter. There were more papers inside the desk, full of numbers and names, and amounts of money. He calmly photographed them, too. When he had finished, he moved away from the desk, his face wet from the heat. And then he saw it: a single golden brown hair lying across the papers.

Immediately he was angry with her. "You do know what he does," he thought. "You lied to me. You're together with him in this big, dirty, arms-drugs deal." At the same time, he was pleased that she was taking the same journey as him, only without Burr or Rooke to help her. But suddenly he was frightened, too. Not for himself, but for Jed. "You stupid woman!" he thought. "Have you ever seen a woman after she has been punched so hard in the face that it killed her?"

Jonathan put the hair carefully in his shirt pocket, and he was pulling out some more papers when he heard the sound of horses outside. Then he heard Jed shouting and Daniel crying.

"Stay calm," he thought.

He put the camera-pen back in his pocket and shut the office door behind him, locking it with the lock pick. He moved quietly through the walk-in cupboard back into the bedroom and heard Jed coming fast and heavily up the stairs in her riding boots. Should he go back into the cupboard? No, hiding wasn't the answer. He *wanted* to meet her. He waited next to the flowers.

When Jed entered, her face was hot and angry. She started speaking as soon as she saw him. "Thomas, please will you teach Daniel not to cry every time he hurts himself! Maybe he will listen to you . . . Actually, Thomas, what are you doing in our room?"

"I brought you some flowers from our climb yesterday," he said.

"Why didn't you give them to the cleaners to put here?" she asked. Then she looked down at the bed and yesterday's clothes, which were lying on a chair. "Flowers or no flowers," she said. "You shouldn't be in here. Get out."

But he was calm, and worried for her, and this made him stronger than her. "Close the door," he said, finally. "There's something I have to say to you."

He looked at her, and he could see that she was not sure. But she closed the door.

"I can't stop thinking about you," he said. "I go to sleep and think about you. I wake up and think about you. A lot of the time I argue with you. I don't understand it. I've never heard you say anything clever. Most of what you say is rubbish. But, every time I think of something funny, I need to share it with you. And when I'm unhappy I need you to make me smile again. But I don't know you at all. I don't know if you're here for Roper's money, or because you love him. And I don't think that you know either."

They were his own words. He was not acting now.

She closed her eyes and was quiet for a few moments. Then she opened them again and touched her face with her hand, as if she had been hit. "That's the rudest thing *anyone* has said to me *ever*," she said. Neither of them spoke.

"Thomas!" she said.

Jonathan said nothing.

"Thomas, this is *Roper's* house!" she said.

"It's Roper's house, and you're Roper's girl. But you don't want to be now, do you?" he said. "Roper is a crook, as I'm sure Caroline Langbourne has told you. He sells arms, and he murders people. That's why people like you and me are watching him and leaving bits of ourselves in his office." He lifted her hair from his pocket. "If he saw your hair on his papers, then he would know that you were in his office. He would kill you for that. That's what he does – he kills."

He waited for her to speak. But she did not move, and her face was very white.

"I'll go and speak to Daniel then," he said. "Where is he?"

———————

That night at 12.30 a.m., he heard someone knock on the door of his cottage in Crystal. "They've come for me," he thought, and he came to the door with a knife in his hand. "She's told them, and now I'm finished." "Hello?" he called from behind the door. He was surprised to hear Jed's voice answer.

He opened the door, and she entered dressed in a dark shirt and skirt.

"Did anyone see you? Caroline? Daniel?" he asked, quickly shutting the door.

"No one," she said. "I was very quiet. No one heard me. Daniel did a painting for me, to say sorry."

"I know, I heard you telling Roper on the phone. What else did you tell him?" said Jonathan.

"Nothing," she said. "What should I tell him? That you called me stupid and him a murderer?" Jonathan did not reply. "How the hell did I get into this?" she said then. "With Roper, I mean."

Then she told him everything: how she had met Roper at the horse sale in France and how he had helped her to escape from a difficult time in her life. "But Caroline's told me that he sells arms," she said. She stared at him. "I'm in a lot of trouble," she said. "I'm a crook's girl. I walked into this with my eyes closed."

Hours later, he took her upstairs to the bedroom and lay next to her, without touching her. He told her who he was and that he was watching Roper as part of an operation. He told her about Sophie.

She left the cottage early in the morning and came back the next night. They talked a lot more about their lives and about Roper, and then they kissed for the first time.

———

Roper returned a week later with Corkoran and Langbourne, and that afternoon they gave Jonathan a new passport with the name Derek S. Thomas on it. Jonathan practised signing the name on a piece of paper. When he was ready, he signed the name in the passport. Langbourne took it, closed it and gave it to Roper.

"I thought it was mine – to keep," said Jonathan.

"Why did you think that?" said Langbourne.

"We've got a job for you," said Roper, in a kinder voice. "After you've done it, you can go."

"What kind of job?" asked Jonathan, carefully.

"We're going to give you a company," replied Roper, smiling. "You'll be travelling and doing a lot of deals. It's exciting, but you'll need to keep it a secret. But first we need you to sign some documents for us."

Roper called his secretary, and she came in with some papers, which she put on the table. They were accounts for a company called Tradepaths. Jonathan signed them.

Then Roper showed him a document that gave him the business, with all the money that Tradepaths owned and had borrowed, and all its risks. Jonathan signed that, too.

_____

"Enjoyed being alone, did we old love?" Corkoran asked him. He was sitting in Jonathan's garden, drinking a beer.

"Very much," replied Jonathan.

"Yes, everyone says you enjoyed it. Tabby says you enjoyed it. Most of the island think you enjoyed it."

He was silent for a moment. Jonathan said nothing. Then Corkoran suddenly said, "Anyway, I have a message from the Boss. It's time to say goodbye to Crystal, and everyone else on it."

"Where am I going?" asked Jonathan.

Corkoran looked at Jonathan as if he hated him. Then he jumped up and turned towards the beach. "To the next meeting, instead of me, that's where you're going! I tell him that you're bad, but he doesn't believe me. He loves you. You saved his boy. Me? I'm just old news. Two nights Jed came to you, I heard. I want to tell him, but he'll kill her, and I don't want that. But *someone* will tell him, old love. Just you wait."

_____

Autumn rain was falling in London as Rex Goodhew decided to go to war. One morning the week before, two drivers in white trucks had nearly killed him while he was riding his bike. Goodhew knew it had been no accident. That same afternoon, he gave Burr's agency ten offices in his government building in Whitehall for the Operation Limpet team to use. The next day, he took away any telephones that the River House could listen to and had all the computers checked.

Every evening after work, he went straight to Burr's office. "I'm going to destroy their Operation Flagship," he told Burr one evening. "You know Harry Palfrey – he's an adviser to the government and knows Darker. Well, he has told me about Flagship. It's a name that Darker and his team have given themselves. If you're not in Flagship, you won't be given any information. But Darker won't have a team left when I've finished with him, and Roper will be safely in prison."

Burr listened to Goodhew's story about the bike and agreed that Geoffrey Darker was trying to **threaten** him. He had been careful himself – driving his children to school in the mornings and getting them in the evenings. "But Goodhew doesn't know how bad the **corruption** really is," he thought later. Three times already, he had been told by Whitehall that he could not see documents that he had asked for.

"You mean they're Operation Flagship!" Burr had shouted at the secretary the third time it happened.

"Operation *what*, sir?" said the secretary.

But the information still came quickly to Operation Limpet from Burr's and Strelski's agents. Roper's deal was definitely happening. Six **container** ships were sailing across the Atlantic Ocean to the island of Curaçao near

Venezuela, to arrive in about a week's time. "Apostoll says that Roper's buying American arms," Strelski told Burr on the phone from Miami. "But we don't know where they will do the exchange." Then, the next day, Strelski rang to give Burr more information. "The cartels are sending their drugs from Buenaventura in Colombia," he said.

Strelski had heard that 100 Colombian army trucks and **tanks** were in Buenaventura – the Colombian government were helping the cartels with the operation! But when he asked for photographs of the tanks he was told that he could not have them. "The CIA cannot give them to us because they are Operation Flagship," he told Burr on the phone.

"Then Flagship includes the CIA, too," Burr thought, angrily.

The next day, Burr got Jonathan's photographs from Roper's office and showed them to Goodhew. Seeing the names of the people included in Roper's deals made Goodhew feel sick. It was not just the corruption of a huge number of important people. It was also the number of big, old companies with good names who were making a lot of money from those deals.

After this, Goodhew stopped trusting anyone, and he started to look at the people in Whitehall with new eyes. "Are you another of them?" he asked himself, quietly, each day as he watched the ministers calmly eating their lunch in the dining room. "Are *you*? Are *you*?"

CHAPTER NINE

In Curaçao

Harry Palfrey was sitting with Rex Goodhew in a North London pub.

"Darker's team haven't threatened you, too, have they?" Goodhew asked. Then he told him about the two trucks.

Palfrey lit a cigarette. "No, but Burr's getting a bit close to Roper," he said. "I told them that it might happen, but they wouldn't listen to me."

"You *told* them?" repeated Goodhew. "Told who?"

"Darker's people. Flagship people. You have to play on both sides, you know, Rex. But they've been listening to my phone and know that I've been speaking to you." He drank his beer quickly.

"So what did you tell them?" asked Goodhew.

Palfrey was quiet for a moment. He did not look at Goodhew. "Darker took me for lunch," he said, finally. "He wants to know that I'm on his side, so he's asked to read my Operation Limpet documents. I have to give them to him by Wednesday 5 p.m."

"Is that all?"

"Why shouldn't it be?" Palfrey replied.

But Goodhew knew that Palfrey was not telling him everything.

"What else did you tell Darker?" Goodhew asked.

Palfrey drank some more of his beer. Then he said,

"I *had* to tell him something, Rex. He wanted information. So I told him that I'd looked at the reports about the cartels, and I'd noticed something about the Greek man."

"You mean you told him about Apostoll?" said Goodhew, quietly.

Palfrey smiled proudly, and for the first time that afternoon he looked relaxed.

"Yes," he said to Goodhew's white face. "I talked about how he's working with the cartels and then selling them to us. Can you believe it?"

———

As soon as Goodhew left the pub he phoned Burr and told him about Apostoll. Burr put down the telephone and stared at the wall. He now had a terrible problem. If Darker's team told the cartels about Apostoll working on both sides, Apostoll would be threatened, **tortured** and made to talk. He might tell them about Jonathan, and then Jonathan could be in danger. Because of Harry Palfrey, Burr now had to choose between finishing the operation and saving Jonathan.

"Roper, in two more weeks you'll be caught," he thought. "I'll know which of those six container ships has the arms, and I'll know the numbers of those containers and the place for the exchange. Jonathan, you're the best source I've ever had. But you're in danger now. If Apostoll is tortured, he could talk about you. Everything will be finished. All our hard work. Gone."

Suddenly the telephone rang. It was Rob Rooke, calling

from Curaçao. He was the agent who was always closest to Jonathan and knew best what he and Roper were doing.

"Roper has just flown in," he said. "Jonathan is with him."

"How did Jonathan look?" asked Burr, quickly.

"He looked well. Good suit. Expensive leather shoes and **suitcase**."

Burr looked down at his desk at the maps of the sea. He remembered all the months of work that were behind them.

"We're continuing with Operation Limpet," he told Rooke.

Burr flew to Miami the next day.

On the plane to Curaçao, Jonathan and Roper had sat together like friends, eating warm bread with jam and drinking fresh orange juice. They had talked and laughed a lot. The bright sun came in through the plane's small windows, and both men looked happy. In the seats behind them sat Tabby and Frisky.

In Curaçao, Roper's party stayed in a beautiful hotel by the sea, with an outdoor restaurant and two beaches. "Relax and enjoy yourself," Roper told Jonathan. So he did. He loved the old town with its pretty old buildings and markets. He loved the Dutch voices and the real people, after the ones at Crystal – people who knew nothing about him and what he was doing. Then, one day, he saw Rooke sitting in a café and reading a newspaper, and it made Jonathan remember with a shock why he was there.

That evening, he had a strange phone call in his hotel room. Frisky was reading a magazine in the corner of his room.

"Sorry, I was looking for another Mr Thomas, in room 22," a voice said. Jonathan knew that it was Rooke.

A little later Jonathan called room 22 and Rooke answered. "This is room 319. I have some **laundry**, please," Jonathan said. Then he went to the bathroom and took some papers that he had hidden behind the toilet. He covered them with a dirty shirt, and put the shirt into a laundry bag. Then he put the bag outside the door of his room. Just before he closed the door, he recognized the woman in the hotel **uniform** who was coming to get the bag. She was one of Rooke's agents.

That night, Roper, Jonathan and Langbourne went to dinner. "There's a new lawyer coming from Caracas," Langbourne told them. While he was speaking, Jonathan noticed Rooke sitting at the table behind them.

"Where is Apo?" asked Roper.

"I don't know. They won't say," replied Langbourne. "But everyone else is ready."

That night, when Jonathan was asleep, the phone rang. It must be Rooke, he thought.

"Jonathan," Jed said, proudly.

He was silent for a moment, knowing he should not speak to her. Then he said, "Get off the phone, Jed! Go to sleep."

But he could not put down the phone, and neither could she. Instead he lay with the telephone next to his ear and listened while she said his name, again and again. "Jonathan, Jonathan, Jonathan."

———————

The next day, Roper, Langbourne and Jonathan had a meeting with Moranti, the new lawyer. Apostoll still could not be found. Moranti was tall and thin, and he watched Jonathan with dark, careful eyes. But Jonathan noticed that his hand was always shaking. It shook as he took Jonathan's passport from Langbourne and copied its information. It shook as he gave the passport back to Jonathan and told him where to sign the papers. When Jonathan had signed lots of different documents, the lawyer gave him a large number of **bearer bonds** with the name of his company, Tradepaths Limited, written on them. Jonathan signed the bonds, too.

When they were finished, they all shook hands.

"I'll just have that passport back," said Tabby to Jonathan as they walked out of the building.

———————

That night, one of Roper's drivers took Roper, Langbourne and Jonathan away from the town. Tabby and Frisky came, too. They went along a long, flat road that had water on one side and huge containers on the other. The driver came to a tall gate and turned the car lights out. Jonathan could see machines, and big ships against the night sky.

A man walked up to their car. "One hour," Langbourne said. Then he passed an envelope full of money through the open window. The gate opened, and they drove forward without lights, past row after row of containers.

"Here," said Langbourne to the driver.

They turned right, and a ship rose out of the sea in front of them. Then they stopped. "Mr Thomas and friends," said Langbourne through the car window to a man with blond hair. "We've come to look at the machines."

They all got out of the car and followed the man with blond hair, who had a gun at his side. He opened a large metal door in the ship and smiled at them dangerously.

They went down into the hold of the ship. There were hundreds of containers with the names of different countries written on them. The side of one of the containers was opened and Jonathan saw the machine guns inside it. "Guns have their own silence," he thought. "The silence of the dead to come."

As Jonathan stared inside the container, Langbourne began to talk excitedly about how the guns worked and how many people they could kill in one minute. There were also missiles in the containers, he said, which could bring down small planes and helicopters.

"Do you like it?" asked Roper, proudly, turning to Jonathan. Their faces were very close.

"It's amazing," Jonathan replied.

"Different guns in each container. A bit of everything."

Then Langbourne called to him. "Thomas!" he shouted. "Come over here. It's signing time."

CHAPTER TEN

An unreal war

In Miami, Burr sat at his small, grey desk in the office he shared with Strelski and thought about Operation Limpet. Everything was going well – everyone said so. Strelski thought it, and so did Goodhew, who phoned him every day from London. "The people at the top agree that Limpet is very important," Goodhew had told him this morning.

"Which people at the top?" asked Burr.

"My minister. He saw your list," said Goodhew.

"Which list?" asked Burr.

"The one that your source photographed," said Goodhew. "The list of people who are doing deals with Roper. Just the names and numbers – not the actual photograph, of course. Roper will think we stole the list from his post, or heard it in a telephone call."

"Roper didn't put that list in a letter!" shouted Burr. "He didn't say it over the phone. He wrote it on a piece of paper, and our source took a photograph of it. Roper will know immediately where those names and numbers came from."

"Don't shout at me, Leonard," replied Goodhew. "My minster is shocked and unhappy about the corruption. Can't you see? And I work for this man, so I have to tell him how we are doing. He wants to have lunch with me on Thursday to tell me some important news. I thought you would be happy, not angry."

Burr breathed slowly. "Yes, of course, I understand, Rex," he said. When he ended the call he immediately rang Rooke. "Rex Goodhew must get no more Limpet reports from us that we haven't checked first," Burr said. "And that's from *now*."

———

Even after that, Burr and Strelski thought that things would be OK. But both were quietly worried when Burr asked the American government if they could stop a ship sailing out of Curaçao to Colón in Panama. "We believe it is carrying arms worth more than fifty million dollars," he told the government. But the answer was no.

Then Burr and Strelski heard that Apostoll had been exchanged for a lawyer called Moranti. "Maybe things were getting too dangerous for him," Burr thought. "He's just decided to stop for a bit." And Moranti lived in Caracas, of course, which was closer to Curaçao. But he was worried when he learned that Sir Anthony Bradshaw had called Roper from England. And after that Strelski got a call from the police.

Strelski left Burr in the office and immediately drove to some expensive Miami apartments called Sunglades, in a rich area where he had never been before. There were lots of police cars there. "We heard you had some interest in this Dr Apostoll," said one of the policemen, whom Strelski knew a little. "That's why we called you. It's bad, sir." Long before he reached the apartment, Strelski knew that Dr Paul Apostoll was dead.

An hour later, Strelski returned to the office with the news that Apostoll had been murdered. He did not look at Burr while he was speaking. Burr knew that Strelski was very angry and that he was thinking, "It's your people who have killed him, and now I wish we weren't sitting in the same room."

Burr's first call was to Rooke in Curaçao, to tell him that Operation Limpet was in danger and that Jonathan needed to be given the **signal** to escape. This meant that he had to get away from Roper and his group and get to the nearest British Embassy.

But the call came too late. When Rooke got Burr's message, he was already watching Roper's plane taking off from Curaçao, on its way to Panama. Then Burr rang Goodhew in London. "Apostoll was tortured before he was murdered," he said. "Perhaps he told them about Jonathan. But if we get Jonathan out, we can still go after Roper. We have a lot more information about him now."

"Oh yes, well I see," replied Goodhew in a strange voice. "Yes, you mustn't stop what you're doing."

"It always used to be *we*," Burr thought. "So what was the important news from the Minister?" he asked.

"Oh, it's good," Goodhew replied, politely. "They're giving me a new job managing a Whitehall Watch group. It's everything we've fought for. But it means I'll have to stop what I'm doing for Operation Limpet, of course."

At that moment another call came in from one of Burr's agents. Roper's plane had gone below the **radar** as it came into Panama. They had completely lost its signal.

"Then where in the hell is it?" Burr shouted.

"Mr Burr, sir," said a boy called Hank. "It disappeared."

———————

On the plane, Roper told Jonathan that they were going to a mountain called Cerro Fábrega in Panama. "I'm about to see what I've come for," thought Jonathan as he sat between Roper and Langbourne on the plane. Tabby and Frisky were behind them. The plane flew down towards the **jungle** below.

After the plane, they took a helicopter back up above the jungle. Jonathan could now see the sea on one side, and banana trees and a yellow road on the other. They landed in a field, with men in army uniforms and carrying guns staring up at them. When the helicopter engine stopped, a small man ran towards them.

"Hi, Manny!" shouted Roper. "Remember Sandy Langbourne? And this is Derek Thomas."

Five or six other rich and confident European men, who Jonathan recognized from their visits to Crystal Island, joined them, and they all followed the small man down a path. Frisky and Tabby walked at the back.

The birds were singing loudly. Suddenly Jonathan heard guns from behind the trees, followed by the sound of a missile. Then there was silence, before the birds began to sing again.

They climbed for several hours under a dark, rainy sky.

They walked past fast rivers and through thick jungle until they came to a large camp where there was just a cook and a few other men. "Many soldiers were trained here," the small man said, "to fight in Panama, Nicaragua, Guatemala and Colombia. Spanish people, Indian people. They were all **trained** well."

The camp was full of animals in **cages**. Sad tigers, silent monkeys and birds with no wings. "Colonel Fernández loves animals very much," explained the small man.

The next day, they met Colonel Fernández, a tall man with dark hair, who led them to another part of the jungle. They stood above a small town that looked as if it was made of wood. There was an airfield next to the town, with lots of old and broken planes in it. "You're going to watch a **battle**," Tabby whispered to Jonathan.

They were taken to a camp, and Jonathan sat around a table with the other guests. Young boys brought them food and drink while they watched an army plane slowly appear from the north. Suddenly some soldiers jumped out of it in **parachutes** and dropped to the ground. Jonathan noticed that there were a couple of men in army uniforms shouting at the soldiers in American voices. Then one of the tanks at the end of the field started shooting at the men with the parachutes, but the men shot back, and suddenly the tank was on fire.

For the next hour, Jonathan and the others watched, amazed, as a huge battle was held in the wooden town in front of them. All kinds of guns and missiles were used to destroy the buildings. Finally a very large passenger plane appeared. "Is it part of the show?" thought Jonathan. "Or is it the CIA?"

Roper laughed when he saw Jonathan's face. "The Russians stole it from an airport," he said. "But a computer is flying it now."

Suddenly a missile was shot into the air and the plane became a ball of fire before disappearing into the jungle. A huge cloud of smoke came up from the trees. As all the men around the table watched with their mouths open, Jonathan carefully took two hundred American dollars from Tabby's pocket and put it in his own. Tabby did not notice that the money was gone.

CHAPTER ELEVEN

Prisoners

Strelski read the copy of the handwritten **fax**, given to him by someone in the CIA who wanted to help Operation Limpet. Still angry with the British after Apostoll's death, Strelski drank a whole bottle of beer. Then he went to the Miami office and gave the fax to Burr.

IMPORTANT

Newbury, England
From Sir Anthony Bradshaw to Richard Roper
  Dear Richard,
About our conversation two days ago – this is to let you know that Dr Paul Apostoll was talking to unfriendly people. They used him to report bad news about Major Corkoran so that you would get a new signer. I hope you will do something about this information quickly. Please send my money through the usual bank.
Best wishes,

  Anthony

Jed and Corkoran left Crystal Island together and flew to Miami. It was the first time in months that Jed had not flown in a private plane, and at first she was excited. "I'm back in ordinary life," she joked to Corkoran, but he just made an angry face. He was angry because Roper had chosen Jonathan to go to Curaçao and not him. But now Roper wanted him again.

Corkoran was rude to Jed again at Miami airport and kept her passport in his pocket. She was hurt because he had never been like this with her before.

While they were waiting for the flight to Antigua, two large blond men came and stood with them.

"Who are they, Corky?" she asked.

"Friends of the Boss, actually," he replied, coldly. "They're coming with us."

And then she saw his eyes and felt scared, because she knew they were extra bodyguards, and this was a Corkoran she did not know.

———

Jonathan was a prisoner now, too. But perhaps he had always been one since he had arrived on Crystal Island.

He first realized that things had changed when Roper and his group were back at the airfield on Cerro Fábrega. The other guests had already left. Langbourne and Moranti were getting on to Roper's plane while Roper was saying goodbye to Colonel Fernández. Suddenly a boy ran up to Roper with a piece of paper. Roper read it, and Jonathan saw an angry look come into his face. Then Roper called Frisky over and whispered something to him.

Frisky took Jonathan's arm and led him on to the plane. He told him to take the seat next to him.

"I've got a bad stomach actually, Frisky," said Jonathan. "I need to be near the toilet."

"You'll sit where you're told," said Frisky. So Jonathan had to sit between him and Tabby, and, when he went to the toilet, Tabby waited outside. Roper sat alone at the front and spoke to no one, except to say thank you for a fax that Jonathan could see was handwritten. Roper read it and put it in his pocket. Then he stared ahead.

When they got to Colón airport in Panama, Jonathan was ordered to sit in the second car between Tabby and Frisky. It was driven by a small Panamanian man who wore a black suit. "I'll need the toilet again soon," Jonathan said to Tabby.

"You need to be quiet," Tabby threatened.

Roper's car drove in front and led them to a beach with tall houses and high gates. Container ships sailed on the water. They drove to a huge building with a picture of a flying bird above the door. The two cars stopped, and they all went inside.

"I really need to use the toilet again," Jonathan told Tabby.

"Well, hurry up then," said Tabby, angrily. They found a toilet, and Tabby and Frisky waited outside. Inside the toilet, Jonathan quickly wrote a note about the building with a bird above the door and put it in an envelope.

Afterwards they followed the others through an office and through another door, which closed behind them. In front of them stood thousands of boxes. Langbourne pointed at one of the boxes, and a boy pulled it out and opened it for him. Roper nodded. About another thirty boxes were opened, and then Jonathan signed for fifty tonnes of Colombian coffee beans.

When they had finished, Roper's group returned to their cars and drove off. But after a few minutes Jonathan asked to stop at a gas station.

"Not again!" said Tabby.

"Go with him, Frisky," Roper called from the first car. "Wait outside the toilet."

Jonathan sat on the toilet and wrote down the numbers of the boxes that he could remember. He added this note to the envelope.

———————

A few hours later, a small Panamanian man in a black suit entered the bar in Panama City where Rooke sat, and gave him two envelopes. "I found these on the floor of my car," the man explained. "Inside one envelope there was a note for me, and some money. The note said that if I brought the other envelope here, I would get five hundred dollars." Rooke opened the first envelope and saw Jonathan's handwritten note in Spanish to the driver. He opened the second envelope and saw Jonathan's list of numbers. Rooke smiled and gave the man five hundred dollars.

———————

When Burr arrived back in London at 8 a.m., he was still wearing his Miami clothes. Goodhew was waiting for him at the airport.

"Any news of Roper's plane?" asked Burr. "Have they found it yet?"

"British Intelligence tell me nothing," replied Goodhew.

"That's twice that my agents have lost that plane in

two days. I don't believe it's a mistake," said Burr. "My source was on it. So were Roper and Langbourne. British Intelligence and the CIA have radar everywhere. How can they lose a thirteen-seat plane?"

"They don't tell me anything, Leonard," replied Goodhew. "They keep me busy and call me the boss of intelligence. But I learn nothing. It's Flagship again – we're not allowed to know. Where's Rooke?"

"He's arriving in London soon," replied Burr.

They waited for a taxi. "Jonathan writes that the arms are on a ship called the *Lombardy*," said Burr. "The cartels are mostly buying American arms with a bit of British as well. Roper is training people to use them, and showing them to his customers at Cerro Fábrega. He also writes that there are American men there in soldiers' uniforms who are doing the training. Rooke thinks that they're CIA. And the drugs are on a ship called the *Horacio Enriques*, sailing from Panama to Gdansk in Poland."

They were in the taxi now. Goodhew stared out of the window. "Think about what you can and can't do, Leonard," he said. "You've got a ship full of arms going to Colombia, and a boat full of drugs going to Poland. You have a crook to catch and a source to save. Don't let Darker and the others stop you from doing that. That's what I did. I was too busy looking at Darker and the list of Roper's friends, and the banks, and Darker again. Forget all that. You can't touch them. Stay with what is possible."

CHAPTER TWELVE

Burr goes to work

The emergency Limpet meeting was planned to start at 10.30 a.m. the next morning at offices in Whitehall, but Rex Goodhew arrived much earlier to check everything was ready and give out documents. He was determined that this would go well, and he knew that he had some important people coming who were on his side. He had told them in a note with Burr's report that they had a battle to fight.

The first people started coming in just before 10.30 a.m. Most of them smiled and shook his hand. More people arrived, including the Minister, and for a while there was talk and laughter. But then suddenly the laughter stopped when Geoffrey Darker appeared and looked around the room with his cold eyes.

They all sat down, and Goodhew started to speak. "Operation Limpet, Minister," he said. "We have some problems, and we need to do something now."

The Minister did not seem happy. "Where's Burr?" he said. "He should be here if this is his report."

Goodhew was pleased to hear this. "He's in the building, sir. I can get him now."

"No," said Darker, loudly. "If we let Burr in, then every agency will want to come to these meetings, and then there will be trouble. We've seen his report – it's enough."

Goodhew was angry, but he could do nothing.

He went on to describe Roper's operation and showed photographs of the SS *Lombardy* and *Horacio Enriques*. "They look like ordinary ships to me," said the Minister. "Why are we worrying about it anyway? It's a Polish problem, isn't it – if it's going to Gdansk? And the *Lombardy* is an American problem."

"Ironbrand is a British company," replied Goodhew. "Its owners are British, the crooks planning the operation are British, and a British agency has done all the work to catch them. Roper has chosen Gdansk because he's probably paying people there. The Poles will do nothing. The drugs will land, and our source will be known."

"Maybe your source is known anyway," said Geoffrey Darker, quietly.

It was the first time that Jonathan had been spoken about.

"That's very possible, Geoffrey," replied Goodhew, slowly. He had never met Jonathan, but he knew what had happened – or was happening – to him. His voice had become very angry. "Limpet has a lot of enemies across the water in the River House. Everyone in the government should be helping us, but they're not. Why is that? Why was I taken away from Operation Limpet? Why does the River House want control of it? 'Everything is Flagship,' they say. But what is Flagship, and why are they controlling important information?"

"Flagship is the American end of this, Rex," said Darker, quietly. "I'm sorry, but it's need-to-know only." Then he asked, "Did the same source who told Burr about the drugs tell him about the arms?"

"Yes," replied Goodhew.

"Is this source's name Jonathan Pine?" Darker asked.

Goodhew said nothing.

"If it's Pine, then he's wanted for stealing and murder, and stolen passports. The police are looking for him. There's also a story that he killed a woman in Cairo. Is this the man that Burr gets his information from, Rex?" asked Darker. "He would do better talking to a drunk person on the street." And now Darker was smiling. "I don't think that the Minster should be asked to listen to Pine's lies. You shouldn't have to either, Rex."

Everyone looked at Goodhew while the Minister started to speak. "Is this true, Rex?" he asked. "Is Pine a murderer, and, if he is, why has Burr used him as a source? There are too many problems. Rex, where are you going? Rex, come back!"

The door seemed a long way, but Goodhew kept walking. "This isn't like you, Rex!" the Minister shouted at Goodhew's back. "You can't make me help you by behaving like this, Rex. Goodbye!"

As soon as Burr heard about the meeting he started working. He was on American time, and his heart was with Jonathan and the pain he knew that he must be feeling. He knew Roper's men must be torturing him to make him speak. He sent his secretary to Whitehall to get the government papers he needed. Then he wrote the letters. Most of them were to himself. A couple were to Goodhew and a couple to Goodhew's minister. He signed each letter with a different name and handwriting.

Then he called Harry Palfrey at the River House. "Come to my office immediately," he said. "I'll explain why when I see you."

Next he phoned Sir Anthony Bradshaw in Newbury, and finally he spoke to Goodhew. "You still have government money to help you with Limpet until the end of the year," Goodhew said in a quiet voice. "So don't stop what you're doing." Then, "That poor boy. What will they do with him? I think of him all the time."

So did Burr, but he had work to do.

Palfrey arrived an hour later and entered Burr's office. Burr stood up and closed the door behind him. Then he punched Palfrey very hard across the face. "That's for Apostoll," he said.

Palfrey sat down on a chair with his hand on his face. "Animal," he whispered.

"I've been good to you, Harry Palfrey, until now," Burr continued, carefully. "I know you have sold Apostoll and Pine to the River House." He took Palfrey's tie and began to pull it hard around his neck. "I'm not feeling good today," Burr said to Palfrey's red face. "It might be because of those men torturing my source. Now I want you to read these papers. As you'll see, Rex Goodhew is not as stupid as you think."

Burr let go of Palfrey's tie and threw some papers marked FLAGSHIP down on his desk. Palfrey read them and began to cry.

Then Burr showed him another paper that had not been signed. It was a paper allowing Burr to send calls to Darker's telephones to other telephones instead, where agents were waiting.

"If you don't sign this, Harry, I will kill you," Burr said. "And after you've signed it, you're going to spend an evening with Rob Rooke in this office. Now sign here; use my pen."

CHAPTER THIRTEEN
Bradshaw makes a call

Soon after Burr's meeting with Palfrey, a message came from Strelski that Jonathan was on the *Pasha*.

"He's alive," Burr thought as he drove through the rain towards Sir Anthony Bradshaw's house in Newbury. "Jonathan hasn't been killed yet because he hasn't told Roper what he wants to know. Roper doesn't know how much Jonathan has told us. He wants to know if he might be **arrested** and how much Flagship can protect him."

"Tell them everything," he told Jonathan in his mind. "Tell them, and then save yourself. Because the enemy's not out there, he's here. *He's us*."

Burr was getting near to Newbury. He drove up a hill and along a road with tall trees on each side. He thought of Rooke and Palfrey sitting in his office, waiting for the phone to ring, and he almost smiled.

He continued up a long road until he reached a huge house that only had lights in its bottom windows. He took his suitcase and walked up the steps to where Sir Anthony Bradshaw was waiting for him.

"That you, Burr?" Bradshaw called.

"Yes."

They went into the house.

"Geoffrey Darker's been arrested," said Burr, immediately.

Bradshaw smiled. "What rubbish! Who arrested him?"

"They're going to arrest Palfrey next," Burr said. "And then you. We've got Roper, too. The police are waiting for his boat to reach land. Rex Goodhew has won this time, Sir Anthony. He's a clever man."

"I don't believe you. I'm going to call Geoffrey at home." Bradshaw picked up the phone. "I want Geoffrey Darker, please," he said after a few seconds. "Sir Anthony Bradshaw would like to speak to him." But Burr knew the call had gone to his own office instead, where Rooke and Palfrey were waiting by the phone.

Bradshaw's face went white as he heard Rooke's answer. "You're *what*?" Bradshaw shouted. "A *policeman*? Where is Geoffrey?"

Next Bradshaw tried phoning the number for Darker's office. This time Harry Palfrey answered. "What do you mean he's not there, Harry?" Bradshaw shouted. And Burr knew Palfrey's reply because he and Rooke had told him what to say.

"*Anthony, get off the phone! Burr and his team have got Geoffrey. The police are here!*"

Bradshaw put down the phone, and his mouth fell open.

Burr opened his suitcase and took out the signed letters marked FLAGSHIP, which he had written earlier. Bradshaw read them through, his face getting white and whiter.

"It's a strange life, isn't it?" Burr said. "You work and work, and nobody wants to know about it. Then suddenly you get a call saying, 'Hey Leonard, why don't you get yourself some hungry young policemen and go and arrest that man Geoffrey Darker? Whitehall is getting too dirty. We want men like him and Anthony Bradshaw to be put in prison. Let the world see what they've done.'"

"Come on," said Bradshaw. "There's no need to arrest me. I'm sure we can do a deal."

Burr smiled. "Yes, we can," he said. "And if you agree to my deal we won't arrest you this time. I want you to call the *Pasha* and speak to our friend, Mr Roper."

"What do you want me to say to him?" asked Bradshaw.

"I want you to tell him that we know what's happening and we are following the *Lombardy* and the *Horacio Enriques* with interest. Tell him that he'll be arrested when his boat reaches land – unless he gives us Pine and Jed. If he agrees, I'll leave him this time. I'll let his ships go where they're going. Darker and Palfrey – they're all going to prison. But not him. And not you. But tell Roper that after this I'll follow him forever, to the ends of the Earth."

CHAPTER FOURTEEN

On the *Pasha*

The day that Jed had arrived in Antigua had been the worst day of her life. At the airport Corkoran had put his hand under her arm and led her to the car. He sat in front, and she sat between the two blond bodyguards in the back. And when she had stepped on to the *Pasha*, the three men had stood around her as she was taken to Roper's office.

Roper was sitting at his desk with his back to her. He was reading something and marking it with a pen. He did not turn or say hello, but continued reading.

She sat down and waited nervously. "Is he going to hit me?" she thought.

"I hear you've been having some fun with Thomas," Roper said, finally, without turning. "You should know that his real name is Pine. Jonathan, to you."

"Where is he?" she asked.

"I thought you'd ask that," answered Roper. He turned a page. "Have you been with him long? You were very good at keeping it secret, even with all those people around. I'm not stupid, but I didn't see it."

"If they're telling you that I've been sleeping with Jonathan, it's not true," she said, quietly. "But yes, I do love him. Is he on the boat?"

Roper did not move. "Pine said he did it all himself. Is that true? He said you didn't do any of it."

"Do any of what?" she asked.

Roper stood up then, but still he did not look at her.

"What are you doing to him?" she said. "Let him go."

Roper turned and walked towards her. He stared at her with cold eyes and said, "I've thought a lot about you, Jed. 'Are she and Pine doing this together?' I thought. 'Corkoran thinks they are.' Is that why I found you at the horse sale? It wasn't just chance."

He touched her face with his hand, and his eyes smiled at her. "I don't know what you're talking about," she said. "You were good to me. And I loved you. You know I did."

"Do you know a man called Burr?" he asked.

"No, I don't know him," she replied.

"That's funny; neither does Pine."

They dressed for dinner then, and their strange nights and days together on the *Pasha* began. They talked about ordinary things in the day, and at night she still slept in his bed. She was always waiting for the moment that he would turn against her, and, at the same time, she knew that she was buying time for Jonathan.

The *Pasha* left Antigua and sailed towards Curaçao. On it were Richard Roper and his guests. They included Lord Langbourne and his wife, Caroline, Major Corkoran, and Jed. There were sixteen other very rich men and women with them, who were there to eat and drink and do deals with Roper. But Jonathan was not with them. He was lying below in the *Pasha*'s dark and bloody hold with chains around his arms and legs. Most of the time he was alone, but sometimes Corkoran came with Tabby and Frisky to **bruise** his face and body even more.

Jed knew where Jonathan was now. She often saw staff from the boat go down some steps into the hold with food. She noticed who visited him and when. It was usually Frisky, Tabby or Corkoran, going in twice a day. "Please, Corky," she said, "tell me how he is. Is he ill? Does he know that I'm on the boat?"

But Corkoran did not tell her anything. Sometimes Langbourne visited him, too, usually in the evening after dinner.

And she knew that Roper also went there, because he was quiet when he came back from that part of the boat. But Jed knew better than to cry or shout. Roper did not like women crying.

———

After Roper's first visit Jonathan had decided not to talk to them at all. He had told Roper that Jed had not helped him, and since then he had said nothing more, not even "good morning" or "hello". He did not want to tell Roper anything about Burr and Rooke and the messages he had sent to them.

But what more *did* Roper want to find out? He knew that Jonathan was an agent and that the stories about his past were not true. He knew enough to change or stop his plans before it was too late. So why was Roper determined to make him talk? Because now, Jonathan decided, he was

Roper's agent. Roper had discovered what he really was, and he needed to control him and, of course, to punish him.

But none of them knew about Sophie. She was there with him every day, speaking to him, making him laugh, telling him to live. While Tabby and Frisky punched his body and he felt terrible pain, Sophie told him how her body had been broken, too. And, of course, she told him to stay silent.

And as the questions continued, Jonathan saw that Roper sometimes came to watch again. "They will kill you, Pine," he said. "Tell them before it's too late."

———

Then something amazing happened. There was a telephone call for Roper in the early evening from Sir Anthony Bradshaw. Roper turned away from Jed to pick up the phone next to the bed, and she saw his back go still. "Anthony, are you crazy?" he said. Then there was a long silence before Roper shouted at her, "Go and have a bath! Close the door, and turn on the water. Do it now!"

A few minutes later he stood by the bathroom door. "You need to get dressed," he said. "Corkoran will be here in two minutes."

———

Frisky and Tabby came for Jonathan at the same time. He thought that this was the end, and that they had finally come to kill him. So, when the two bodyguards opened the door and took off his chains, he was ready for them.

"We've had enough of you, Thomas," said Tabby. "So now you're going on a journey."

They carried him up from the bottom of the boat, and he looked up at the stars. He looked down at the water, and he could see land nearby – there were house lights, and cars on a road. Then he saw Roper wearing a white jacket and trousers. Corkoran was there, too, and between them he could see Jed.

Jonathan suddenly took both Tabby and Frisky's heads and hit them together very hard. The men screamed and fell to the ground. Corkoran lifted his gun and Roper said, "That was a very stupid thing to do, Pine."

"Jonathan, look!" Jed shouted. Jonathan looked away from Corkoran's gun and at the same time heard Roper slowly counting. Then he saw that Roper was holding a gun to Jed's head. Jonathan knew he could do nothing to help her. He was very tired, and his body felt broken as he fell down on the deck. This time he heard Jed and Sophie together, shouting at him to stay awake.

When he woke up, they were pulling him to the side of the ship. Corkoran made Jed go first, and then they helped Jonathan down the steps and lifted him into the small boat after her. Jed looked up and saw Roper in his white jacket staring down at her as if he was looking for something he had lost. For a moment, he looked like she remembered him in Paris – a nicely dressed, charming Englishman. Then he moved back from the side of the ship and disappeared.

It was two brothers who noticed the light in the cottage first as they drove past Lanyon Head one night on the way home from their fishing boat. "Who's living in Jack Linden's place now?" one asked.

"Perhaps Jack is back," replied the other.

They did not speak about it again until a week later, when they were standing by the sea and saw smoke coming from the cottage. A man with a big beard came out of the front door. It was Jack, they agreed. "More beard than hair!" they joked. But when they told Mrs Trethewey that Jack had come back to Cornwall, she just laughed. "He's no more Jack Linden than I am," she said. "That's a man from Ireland with his girlfriend. They're going to keep horses there and paint pictures. They've bought the cottage. Yes, he looks a bit like Jack, I agree. But I've had the police here. A nice man called Burr came all the way from London and spoke to us about him, and it's fine. So please don't talk badly again of what's happening in that house, because, if you do, you'll hurt two very good people."

During-reading questions

Write the answers to these questions in your notebook.

1 What does Sophie want Jonathan to do for her?
2 Why isn't Freddie Hamid happy?

1 Who is Mr Quayle, do you think?
2 Why are Leonard Burr and Jonathan meeting?

1 After he meets Burr, Jonathan's life changes. How does it change?
2 What is Operation Limpet?
3 Why doesn't Burr want to tell the River House people about Jonathan?

1 What does Burr want Apostoll to do for them?
2 Why does Jonathan get the job at Mama Low's, do you think?

1 Why is Burr happy when he hears Corkoran ask Bradshaw about Jonathan?
2 How does Jed think that Roper makes his money?
3 How does Corkoran feel about Jonathan? How do you know this?

1 How do we know that Roper might not trust Jonathan?
2 How does Roper make Jonathan stay on the island?

CHAPTER SEVEN

1 How does Jonathan feel about Jed?
2 How does Jonathan contact Burr from Crystal Island?
3 "Roper's not very happy with Corky at the moment," Jed tells Jonathan. Why do you think this is?

CHAPTER EIGHT

1 Why does Jonathan think that Jed has become quiet?
2 What does Jonathan find in Roper's office?
3 What dangerous information does Corkoran know about Jonathan?
4 What is Operation Flagship?

CHAPTER NINE

1 What did Harry Palfrey tell Geoffrey Darker? Why is Burr worried about this, and what does he decide?
2 How does Jonathan pass information to Rooke in Curaçao?

CHAPTER TEN

1 What did Goodhew show his minister, and why was Burr angry about this?
2 What things begin to worry Burr and Strelski about Operation Limpet?
3 What does Jonathan watch on Cerro Fábrega?

CHAPTER ELEVEN

1 Why have Jonathan and Jed become prisoners, do you think?
2 Why does Jonathan keep saying that he needs the toilet?
3 What advice does Goodhew give Burr?

CHAPTER TWELVE

1 What is the real reason that Darker does not want Burr in the meeting, do you think? Why is this bad for Jonathan?
2 Why does Goodhew leave the meeting?
3 What does Burr make Harry Palfrey do for him?

CHAPTER THIRTEEN

1 "Tell them, and then save yourself. Because the enemy's not out there, he's here. He's us," Burr tells Jonathan in his mind. What does he mean?
2 What does Burr want Bradshaw to do?

CHAPTER FOURTEEN

1 What does Roper want to know about Jed?
2 What do Jonathan and Jed do after they leave the *Pasha*?

After-reading questions

1 Look at "Before-reading question 5". What have you learned about the CIA and British Intelligence?
2 Why did Roper need a signer, do you think?
3 Which parts of the story that Jonathan tells Corkoran in Chapter Six are true, and which parts are false, do you think?
4 Did Jed really love Roper, do you think? Did Roper really love Jed? Give reasons for your answers.
5 Did Burr manage to stop Roper in the end, do you think?
6 How "real" is the story of *The Night Manager*, do you think? Are there people like Roper in this world, and is there corruption in governments and big companies that helps others like him?

Exercises

CHAPTER ONE

1 **Match the words to the definitions in your notebook.**

Example: 1—b

1	staff	**a**	an important person in the government
2	minister	**b**	They work for a person or a business.
3	charming	**c**	things like guns and bombs
4	arms	**d**	when there are no sounds or noise at all
5	missile	**e**	something that is used to damage a place
6	bruised	**f**	saying and doing nice things
7	silence	**g**	when your skin has marks on it because someone or something hit you

CHAPTER TWO

2 **Write the correct names in your notebook.**

> Jemima Marshall (Jed)   Jonathan Pine
> Major Corkoran (Corky)   Frisky   Lord Langbourne
> Leonard Burr   Apostoll (Apo)   Richard Roper

1 .*Jemima Marshall (Jed)*. is from England. She is young and beautiful and Richard Roper's girlfriend.

2 .... is a dealer and lives in Nassau.

3 .... is the night manager of the hotel.

4 .... is one of Richard Roper's bodyguards.

5 .... signs everything for Roper and looks after the group's passports.

6 .... is very handsome and is married to a woman called Caroline.

7 .... manages an agency that helps British Intelligence.

8 .... is a lawyer who works for the drugs cartels.

CHAPTER THREE

Complete these sentences with the correct form of the verb in your notebook.

1 After their meeting, he did everything Burr ..*had*.. (have) told him to do.

2 Mrs Trethewey called upstairs to her daughter .... (tell) her that a nice young man had come to stay in the village.

3 A couple of months later Jack Linden .... (see) in Falmouth talking to a large Australian man in a bar.

4 There was lots of blood .... (find) at the cottage.

5 "During the last eight years," said Strelski, "different groups – .... (include) French, Israelis and Cubans – have tried to sell arms to these Columbian cartels."

CHAPTER FOUR

Write questions for these answers in your notebook.

1 Where .*did Strelski land the plane*.?
He landed it on a small airfield that had cows on one side.

2 Why ....?
Because Roper is charming and confident, and he has big plans.

3 Who ....?
Major Corkoran signed them.

4 What ....?
A list of all the bad things that Corkoran did before he met Roper.

5 Why ....?
Burr told Jonathan to save Daniel because he wanted Roper to trust Jonathan and bring him into his team.

CHAPTER SIX

5 **Who is thinking this, do you think? Write the correct names in your notebook.**

> Jonathan   Corkoran   Roper

1 "I will tell them some things that are true, and some things that are lies." .....*Jonathan*......
2 "He's very confident and charming. I could like him if I didn't hate him because of Sophie."
3 "I can't leave this island. They have my passport!"
4 "I'm going to find out everything about him that I can, and then report to the Boss."
5 "I'm going to use him to make money for me instead of Corkoran."

CHAPTER SEVEN

6 **Complete these sentences in your notebook, using the words from the box.**

> kept   promised   dealer   row   except

1 Roper .....*kept*.... his promise and gave Jonathan a little cottage on the other side of Crystal Island.
2 "You can have any woman here .... Jed," Corkoran told Jonathan.
3 He carried on up until he came to a .... of old houses.
4 "But this is what you .... me, isn't it?"
5 Roper talked on the phone a lot – to the captain of the *Pasha*, or to his antiques .... in London.

CHAPTER TEN

7 Write the correct question word in your notebook.
Then answer the questions.

1 ...*What*... did the people at the top think about Limpet?

2 .... photographed the list?

3 .... will Roper know that Jonathan stole the list?

4 .... lawyer was Apostoll exchanged for?

5 .... had Burr's call to Rooke come too late?

6 .... can't they find Roper's plane?

7 .... did the soldiers land from the plane?

8 .... much money did Jonathan steal from Tabby?

Project work

1 Write about the people in the story. Who is good, and
who is bad? Are there some characters who are both good
and bad? Give reasons for your ideas.

2 Write a newspaper report about the murder of the
Australian man in Cornwall.

3 Write a letter from Jed to Jonathan at the end of
Chapter Nine.

An answer key for all questions and exercises can be found at
www.penguinreaders.co.uk

Glossary

adviser (n.)
someone whose job is to give advice to a person or *government*

agency (n.)
in this story, a group of people who work together to try to learn secret things about another country

agent (n.)
a person who tries to learn secret things about another country

airfield (n.)
a place where planes can fly from and land. It is smaller than an airport.

antique (n. and adj.)
An *antique* is something that is old and worth a lot of money.

arms (pl. n.)
things like guns and bombs that countries use to attack each other

arrest (v.)
If someone is *arrested*, the police stop them and take them away to a police station.

battle (n.)
a fight between two armies in a war

bearer bond (n.)
a document that says an amount of money will be paid to the person who has the document

bodyguard (n.)
someone whose job is to watch an important person and stop people from attacking them

boss (n.)
a person who tells other people at work what they must do. *Boss* can also be used as a name when you are talking to the person who tells you what to do at work.

break in (phr. v.); **break-in** (n.)
to enter a room that you should not be in by breaking a *lock*, window, etc. Someone might do this so that they can secretly look for something or steal something.

British Embassy (pr. n.)
a building where people work for the British *government* in a foreign country

British Intelligence (pr. n.)
the group of people who try to discover secret information about foreign countries for the British *government*

bruised (adj.); **bruise** (v.)
If you *bruise* part of your body, someone or something hits you and makes a mark on your skin. Your skin is *bruised*.

cage (n.)
a place with bars (= long thin pieces of metal or wood) on all sides. People put animals in *cages*. Then the animals cannot move to another place.

cards (n.)
a game played with 52 *cards* (= small pieces of strong paper) with numbers and pictures on them. People sometimes try to win money by playing *cards*.

cartel (n.)
a group of people who work together so that they can sell something at the highest price and try to stop other people from selling it

charming (adj.)
If someone is *charming*, you like them because they say and do nice things.

CIA (Central Intelligence Agency) (pr. n.)
a part of the United States *government* that collects secret information about people and organizations

confident (adj.)
Someone who is *confident* knows that they can do things very well.

container (n.)
a large metal box with things inside it. *Containers* are put on to ships and taken to other countries.

corruption (n.)
when important people in a company or *government* are not honest and do bad things

cottage (n.)
a small house in the countryside (= an area that is not a town or city)

crook (n.)
a person who is not honest and does bad things. For example, they might steal things or kill people.

dealer (n.); **deal** (n.)
A *dealer* is a person who sells things. A *deal* is when you agree to sell something at a price.

destroy (v.)
to damage something so much that it is completely broken or cannot continue

determined (adj.)
showing that you want to do something and will not let anyone stop you from doing it

drug (n.)
People take *drugs* to feel happy, excited, etc. Buying and selling *drugs* is against the law.

exchange (v. and n.)
when you give something to a person and they give something to you at the same time

fax (n.)
a message on a piece of paper that has been sent from a machine in one place and comes out of a machine in another place. The information is sent using a telephone line.

government (n.)
a group of important people who decide what must happen in a country

helicopter (n.)
A *helicopter* is like a small plane, with long, thin metal parts on top of it.

hold (n.)
the part of a ship where all the *containers* are. The *hold* is below the floor that people walk on.

include (v.)
to have something or someone as part of a larger group

jungle (n.)
a hot and wet place where there are a lot of trees and plants growing closely together

land (v.)
to arrive on the ground after a journey in a plane or *helicopter*. When a person *lands* a plane, they make it go down to the ground.

laundry (n.)
clothes that need to be washed

lawyer (n.)
A *lawyer* helps people with the law.

leather (n.)
the skin from an animal, which is used for making clothes and furniture

limousine (n.)
a very long, expensive car

list (n.)
things like names or numbers that have been written one below the other

lock (v. and n.)
If you *lock* a door, you close it with a key. A *lock* is the part of a door that you put the key into.

lock pick (phr.)
something that you put into a *lock* to try to open a door when you do not have a key

minister (n.)
an important person in the *government*

missile (n.)
something that is used to damage a place. *Missiles* are shot from something and can travel a long way.

operation (n.)
When a spy works on an *operation*, they take part in a planned activity.

parachute (n.)
When people jump out of a plane, they use a *parachute* that suddenly opens and helps them fall slowly and safely.

passport (n.)
a document that has your photograph and shows your name and when you were born. You need a *passport* to travel to a foreign country.

photocopier (n.)
a machine that can make copies of a document

protect (v.)
to look after someone and stop bad things from happening to them

punch (v.)
to hit someone hard with your fist
(= closed hand)

radar (n.)
something that is used to find the
position of planes or ships and watch
their movement. It works using radio.

reception (n.)
the place where you go when you
arrive at a hotel

risk (n.)
something you do that might have
bad results

robber (n.)
a person who tries to steal something
from someone

safe (n.)
a strong metal box with special
locks. You keep things like money or
important documents in it.

sale (n.)
when you sell something

signal (n.)
an action or message that tells
someone something.

silence (n.)
when there are no sounds or noise
at all

source (n.)
a person who secretly gives
information to someone else. They
are the *source* of the information.

staff (n.)
Staff work for a person or a business.

suitcase (n.)
a large box or bag that you put your
clothes in when you travel

tank (n.)
a large, strong machine with a gun
on the top. Soldiers use it to move
over ground that is not flat.

team (n.)
a group of people who are working
together

terrace (n.)
a flat place outside a house or
restaurant where you can sit or eat

threat (n.); **threaten** (v.)
A *threat* is someone or something that
is dangerous and may hurt you. If a
person *threatens* you, they make you
think that they will do something
bad to you if you do not do what
they want.

torture (v.)
to hurt someone or do bad things to
them until they do or say what you
want. People are usually *tortured* for
information.

training (n.); **train** (v.)
to teach someone how to do a job or
how to use something

uniform (n.)
the clothes that all people working
for a company must wear